W9-AYN-760

The
STEADFAST
T ★ I ★ N
SOLDIER

The
STEADFAST
T★I★N
SOLDIER

By Hans Christian Andersen
Retold by Simon Lewin

DISNEP
PRESS
NEW YORK

With Illustrations from the Disney Archives

Text and illustrations copyright © 1991 Disney Press. All rights
reserved. No part of this book may be used or reproduced in any
manner whatsoever without written permission of the publisher.
Printed and bound in the United States of America. For information
address Disney Press, 114 Fifth Avenue, New York, New York
10011. The stories, characters, and/or incidents in this publication
are entirely fictional.

1   3   5   7   9   10   8   6   4   2

Library of Congress Catalog Card Number: 91-71342

ISBN: 1-56282-016-8/1-56282-073-7 (lib. bdg.)

There was once a company of brave tin soldiers, twenty-five in all, and all brothers, since they had been cast from the same mold. They were dashing indeed in their tall hats and elegant uniforms, as alike as so many peas in a pod.

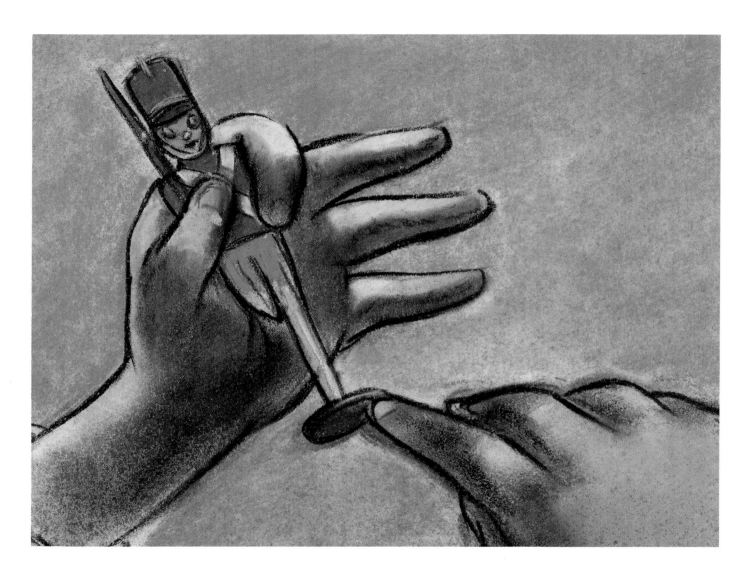

All, that is, except for one who lacked a leg. He was the last to have been cast, and the tin had run out before he could be finished. But this brave little soldier was always good humored and never complained.

The soldiers were kept on a table in the playroom of some very fortunate children. The table was shared by many other marvelous toys, none more wonderful than a little ballet dancer. She was cut out of paper and lived in a castle set in the middle of the table.

She wore a charming costume of delicate white silk, with a red tinsel rose at her waist.

Being a dancer, she kept her arms raised gracefully and stretched a leg so far behind her that she, too, appeared to have but one leg.

The tin soldier would often stare at the beautiful dancer for hours, dreaming that one day she might become his wife. Although he knew this was hardly likely (for she lived in a fine castle, while he shared a common box with his twenty-four brothers), it did not keep the good-hearted soldier from dreaming.

If the children of the house had been good, they were allowed to play with their toys for a while after supper. Then the toys were put neatly away, and the children were sent to bed.

As the evening wore on, the house became more and more quiet, as people and toys slept. Then, at the stroke of midnight, there would be a sudden stirring in the playroom as the toys came magically to life.

The box in which the soldiers lived would open. Then each one, as if on command, would rise to attention and begin to march behind the little military band as it began the *rum-pum-pum* of a lively martial tune.

It was difficult, of course, for the one-legged soldier to get out of the box. He worked hard though and, after a bit of fumbling and stumbling, would manage to right himself. I think it's getting easier each time I try, he would say to himself as he hurried to join the others.

On this particular evening, as always, he stared with admiration at the little dancer as she dipped and twirled, balanced on only one leg. Like all performers, she loved having an audience, and as the soldier watched, she danced more brilliantly than ever. She liked this little soldier very much indeed, and she was glad of his devotion.

Suddenly, there was a very loud *click!* as the lid of a carved wooden box flew open. Out sprang a great ugly green imp of a jack-in-the-box. He was jealous of the attention the tin soldier was receiving and screamed at him, "Stop staring at her, and stop dreaming what you're dreaming! If she won't belong to me, she won't belong to anyone!"

The steadfast tin soldier held his ground, pretending not to hear, refusing to be bullied, unwavering in his love. The imp, enraged, pulled back and sprang out again with all the force he could muster.

The soldier was knocked off balance and fell into the path of a model train that was just speeding by. He was struck so hard by the train that he was thrown onto the windowsill at the end of the playroom and then out the window.

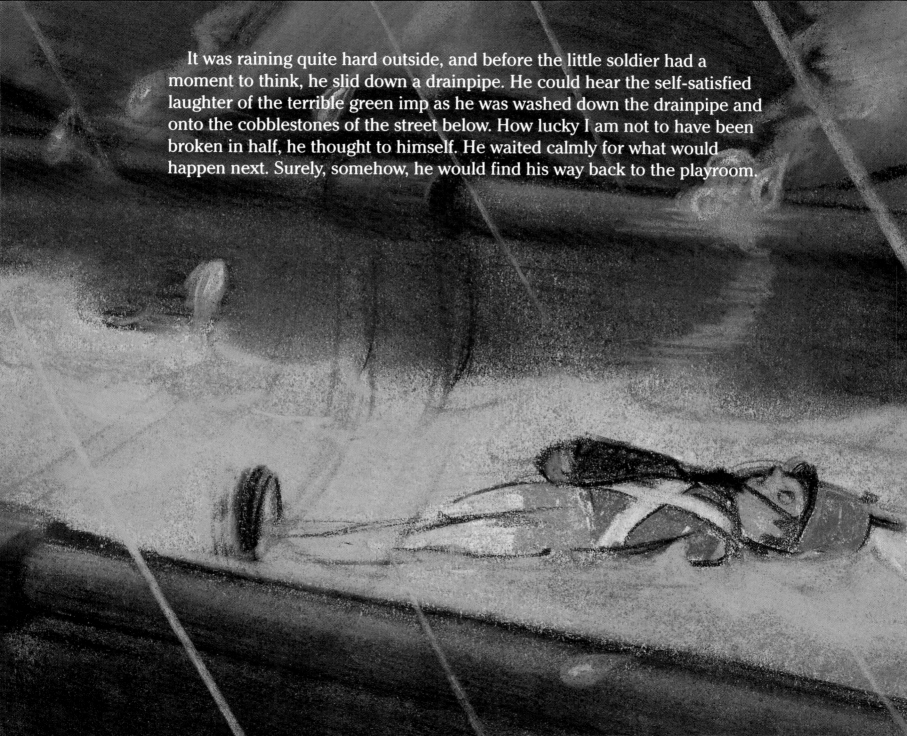

It was raining quite hard outside, and before the little soldier had a moment to think, he slid down a drainpipe. He could hear the self-satisfied laughter of the terrible green imp as he was washed down the drainpipe and onto the cobblestones of the street below. How lucky I am not to have been broken in half, he thought to himself. He waited calmly for what would happen next. Surely, somehow, he would find his way back to the playroom.

The next morning a young boy found the tin soldier in the street where he had fallen. Not much good for marching with only one leg, thought the boy, so he made a little boat from a sheet of newspaper and set the soldier in it.

Rainwater still flowed along the gutters, and the boy quickly set boat and soldier a-sailing. The boy followed along, enjoying the sight, until the boat suddenly sailed through a grating and plunged into the darkness of a sewer.

The soldier could barely see. If only the little dancer were here with me, it could be twice this dark and I wouldn't care, he said to himself.

As he sailed on through the murky tunnels, he barely escaped being overturned by water gushing from a drainpipe and just missed being sucked into a whirlpool. How fortunate I am, he thought as he avoided each disaster. And what an adventure I'm having. I can hardly wait to tell the dancer all about it.

On he went until, after a while, he found himself surrounded by a host of little lights blinking on and off in the dark. Only they weren't lights at all, but the eyes of a troop of hungry water rats! The rats scurried this way and that, trying everything they could to get to the little soldier.

Some even boarded an empty bottle in an effort to block his path, but the bottle sank, and the rats had to swim for their lives. Throughout it all, the steadfast little soldier never flinched, trusting that his boat was seaworthy and the current swift enough to outdistance the rats.

Finally, the tin soldier could see light at the end of the tunnel. How happy he was . . . until he realized that the tunnel emptied out, with a great rush, into the sea.

Into the swirling water he went, trying bravely to keep his boat afloat. But finally, after much buffeting, the boat filled with water, and the paper of which it was made fell to pieces.

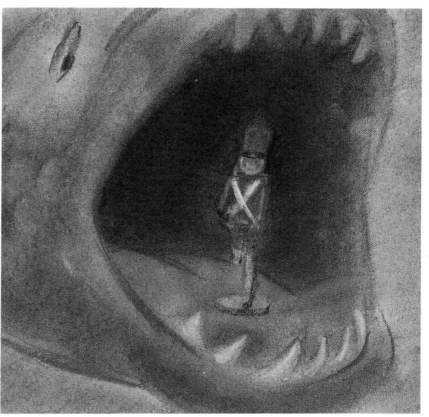

The little soldier fell through the green water, surrounded by a hundred varieties of undersea plants and surely as many little fish who swam up close to investigate him. The steadfast soldier never batted an eye. He watched the seascape as he floated toward the bottom.

Suddenly, all the little fish scattered as a toothy monster appeared and, in one great gulp, swallowed the little tin soldier!

It was even darker inside the fish than it had been in the tunnel, and a lot more cramped. But as the little soldier lay there, he thought of nothing but his beloved dancer. He hoped she was not in the clutches of the wicked green imp.

After a while the great fish was caught, taken to market, and sold for a family's dinner. When the cook picked it up by its tail and began to prepare it for the evening meal, something fell out of its mouth. It was the little tin soldier, of course.

How amazing it was, everyone in the household agreed, that the soldier had survived being eaten by the fish. And more amazing still, that he had been returned to the same house from which he had disappeared! But this did not surprise the little soldier, who had steadfastly refused to believe that he would never see the little dancer again.

And so it was that the tin soldier was returned to the table in the children's playroom. There he stood at attention once more, gazing again with love at the beautiful dancer still balancing on one leg in front of her castle. She, too, was steadfast.

As the clock struck midnight, the little dancer began to move. She was overjoyed to see the soldier again, and she danced closer and closer to him. Then, there was a loud *click!*, and out of the carved box popped the terrible green imp.

He was more angry than ever when he saw that his rival had miraculously returned, and the imp struck him such a vicious blow that the soldier was sent sailing through the air and into the fire that burned in the grate.

The tin soldier stared through the flames at the little dancer. She gazed back at him, and he could feel himself melting from the heat. Still he stood steadfastly at attention, shouldering his gun, smiling at his ladylove.

Suddenly, the window was thrown open by a gust of wind.

The draft caught the little dancer, and she flew like a bird into the fireplace.

There she stood by the tin soldier's side! The two of them had never been so happy. But the dancer was ablaze, and in an instant she was gone.

The next morning, when the maid came to clean the ashes from the fireplace, she found a little tin heart, all that was left of the steadfast tin soldier. In the middle of the tin heart lay a tiny tinsel rose.